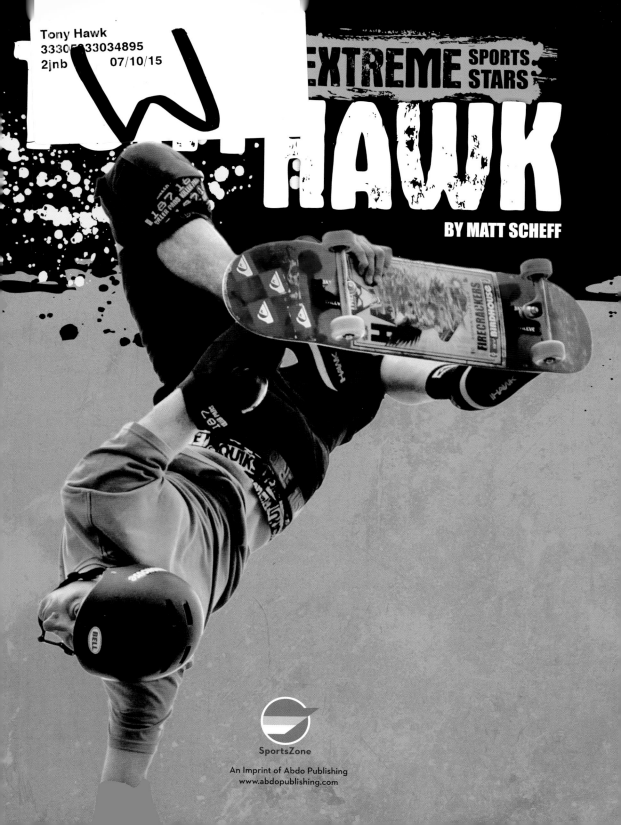

EXTREME SPORTS STARS

HAWK

BY MATT SCHEFF

SportsZone

An Imprint of Abdo Publishing
www.abdopublishing.com

www.abdopublishing.com

Published by Abdo Publishing, a division of ABDO, PO Box 398166,
Minneapolis, Minnesota 55439. Copyright © 2015 by Abdo
Consulting Group, Inc. International copyrights reserved in
all countries. No part of this book may be reproduced in
any form without written permission from the publisher.
SportsZone™ is a trademark and logo of Abdo Publishing.

Printed in the United States of America,
North Mankato, Minnesota
042014
092014

 THIS BOOK CONTAINS
RECYCLED MATERIALS

Cover Photos: Paul A. Hebert/Invision/AP Images
(foreground); Rex Features via AP Images (background)
Interior Photos: Zuma Press/Icon SMI, 1, 28-29;
Tony Donaldson/Icon SMI, 4-5, 31; Kirsty Umback/
Corbis, 6-7; Splash News/Newscom, 8-9; Tao-Chuan
YEH Agence France Presse/Newscom, 10; Tony
Donaldson/Icon SMI, 11; Dustin Snipes/Icon SMI,
12-13; Wireimage/Icon SMI, 14, 15; Newport Daily
News/Dave Hansen/AP Images, 16; Rachel Ritchie/
Newscom, 17; Tony Donaldson/Icon SMI 558/
Newscom, 18-19, 20, 21, 24; PRNewsFoto/Sirius/
AP Images, 22-23; Chris Polk/AP Images, 25, 30
(left); Aaron Harris/AP Images, 26-27, 30 (right)

Editor: Chrös McDougall
Series Designer: Maggie Villaume

Library of Congress Control Number: 2014932900

Cataloging-in-Publication Data
Scheff, Matt.
 Tony Hawk / Matt Scheff.
   p. cm. -- (Extreme sports stars)
Includes index.
ISBN 978-1-62403-453-4
1. Hawk, Tony--Juvenile literature. 2. Skateboarders--United
States--Biography--Juvenile literature.   I. Title.
796.22/092--dc23
[B]
                              2014932900

CONTENTS

Tony skates at the
1999 X Games.

THE 900

Tony Hawk stood atop the halfpipe at the 1999 X Games. A huge crowd had gathered to watch him in the best trick event. Tony wanted to become the first skateboarder ever to land a 900 in competition. To do it, he would need to spin around two and a half times in the air before landing safely.

Tony started down the ramp and built up some speed. Then he launched into the air and spun two and a half times. And then he fell.

Although long retired from competing, Tony could still do amazing tricks at an event in 2012.

FAST FACT

Tony was 31 when he landed his 900 in 1999. He could still do the trick 12 years later, at age 43!

Tony tried again and again. But he kept falling. Soon, he ran out of time. He would not earn an official score, but Tony kept going.

On his eleventh try, Tony finally did it. The crowd roared as he did two and a half spins and then landed safely on his board. The 900! Tony proved once again why he was the greatest skateboarder of all time.

EARLY LIFE

Anthony Frank Hawk was born May 12, 1968, in San Diego, California. He was the youngest of four children. As a kid, Tony had a lot of energy. His mom described him as "challenging." When Tony was nine, his older brother gave him a skateboard. At first, Tony did not even know how to turn. But soon, the skateboard became a perfect way for Tony to burn off energy.

Tony performs for a film crew in 2006 in Venice Beach, California.

FAST FACT

Tony once scored 144 on an IQ test. That is well above average.

Tony flies above BMX biker Mat Hoffman at a 2000 event in Taiwan.

正至中大

Tony learned quickly. He spent a lot of time at a nearby skate park. Tony loved to learn new tricks. He would try them again and again until he mastered them. Tony was often covered in bruises and scrapes. He fell so hard he lost teeth four different times. But he never stopped trying. He said that finally mastering a new trick made it all worthwhile.

Tony in action at the 2000 X Games

Tony started entering amateur skateboarding competitions. Soon, he was too good for amateur events. At age 14, Tony started entering professional competitions. Within two years, he was one of the best skateboarders in the world.

The 1980s were a great time for skateboarding. Tony traveled around the country. His sponsors paid him to use their gear. Tony was making so much money that he bought a house while he was still in high school!

Tony goes upside down while performing a trick at the 2007 X Games.

FAST FACT

In 1986, Tony appeared in the skateboarding film *Thrashin'*. He has been in many more films since then.

Around 1991, Tony was at the height of his skill. But interest in skateboarding was dropping. Fans stopped coming to events. Skateboard companies stopped sponsoring skateboarders. Tony struggled to make a living.

Tony never gave up the sport he loved. He and a friend even started their own skateboarding company, Birdhouse Projects. They later changed the name to Birdhouse Skateboards.

Tony skates outside the Ed Sullivan Theater for The Late Show with David Letterman *in 2002.*

*Tony takes a break
from skating while
on The Late Show
with David Letterman
in 2002.*

The X Games offered an outlet for extreme sports such as skateboarding, inline skating, and BMX biking.

In 1995, the ESPN network put on the first Extreme Games. The event was renamed the X Games the next year. The X Games had competitions in extreme sports such as skateboarding, inline skating, and BMX. The event helped spark a new interest in skateboarding.

The first Extreme Games were much smaller than today's event. The only skateboarding event was the vert. Tony won the event to claim the first skateboarding gold medal in X Games history.

Tony competes in a street event at the 1998 X Games.

FAST FACT

By age 25, Tony had entered 103 pro skateboarding contests. He had won 73 of them and finished second in 19 others!

The X Games got bigger and bigger. Their popularity helped make Tony famous around the world. Tony took second place in the 1996 vert event. His friend Andy Macdonald earned gold. But Tony came back in 1997 to reclaim the gold medal.

FAST FACT

Tony and Andy Macdonald teamed up in 1997 to win the first X Games vert doubles event.

Tony, top, *and Andy Macdonald warm up for their winning run at the 2000 X Games.*

Tony performs a trick in 2000.

BIG BUSINESS, BIG STAR

Tony was bigger than ever after landing his 900 at the X Games in 1999. Then he surprised everyone by retiring. He said he was done skating in competitions. Tony was not retiring from skating completely. He continued touring and putting on demonstrations. But he wanted to focus on new things. That included Birdhouse Skateboards. Tony's business was taking off.

Tony in 2000

SCORE: 7059 SPECIAL SWITCH

A screenshot from Tony Hawk's American Wasteland, a 2005 follow-up to Tony's popular video game

1,854 X 3
SWITCH NOSE MANUAL + SWITCH
WRAP AROUND

In 1999, Tony teamed up with Activision to create a skateboarding video game. *Tony Hawk's Pro Skater* was a huge hit. *Tony Hawk's Pro Skater 2* came out a year later. In all, the series has included more than a dozen games.

According to *Guinness World Records, Tony Hawk's Pro Skater 2* is the highest-selling action-sports video game in history.

A LIVING LEGEND

Tony might have officially retired, but he did not stop skateboarding. And he came out of retirement to skate in special events such as the X Games. In 2003, he won the best-trick gold medal when he landed the 900 before time ran out.

In 2000, he began organizing Tony Hawk's Gigantic Skatepark Tour. He and many of the sport's biggest stars traveled around the country to show off their tricks.

Tony reacts after completing the 900 at the 2003 X Games.

Tony skates in the vert competition at the 2003 X Games.

Tony also devoted a lot of his time to charity work. He started the Tony Hawk Foundation in 2002. Since then, the foundation has helped to build more than 450 skate parks around the United States. Tony is active in the foundation. One of his goals is to encourage young people to live active lifestyles.

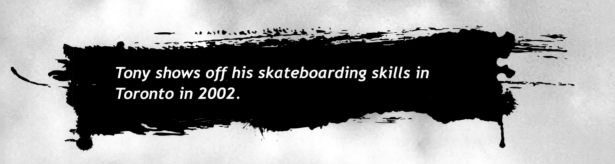

Tony shows off his skateboarding skills in Toronto in 2002.

Tony's competitive days as a skateboarder are behind him. But his influence on the sport lives on. He remains active in the sport that he helped build, encouraging new generations of skateboarders to master bigger and better tricks. Fans might never see Tony perform his famous 900 again. But he still remains one of the biggest stars in the history of action sports.

FAST FACT

Tony wrote and released his autobiography *Hawk: Occupation, Skateboarder* in 2001.

Tony shows off his skills on a halfpipe in 2011.

TIMELINE

1968

Tony is born on May 12 in San Diego, California.

1977

Tony receives his first skateboard from his older brother.

1986

Tony appears in the film *Thrashin'*.

1992

Tony and friend Per Welinder start their own skateboarding company, Birdhouse Projects.

1995

Tony wins the vert event at the first Extreme Games (now X Games).

1999

Tony lands the 900 at the X Games. He retires later that year.

2000

Tony organizes Tony Hawk's Gigantic Skatepark Tour.

2003

Tony wins his tenth and final X Games gold medal by landing the 900 in best trick.

GLOSSARY

amateur
A person who is not paid
to compete in a sport.

charity
An organization that provides
a service to people in need.

halfpipe
A U-shaped ramp used
in skateboarding.

professional
A person who is paid to
compete in a sport.

retire
To stop doing something
as a full-time job.

sponsor
A company that pays an athlete
to use and promote its products.

vert
Short for vertical; in
skateboarding, vert is a type
of event held on a halfpipe
with tall, vertical walls.

INDEX